STINKY and JINKS

My Hamster is a
DETECTIVE

BY DAVE LOWE

D1080875

A TEMPLAR BOOK

First published in the UK in 2014 by Templar Publishing,
an imprint of The Templar Company Limited,
Northburgh House, 10 Northburgh Street, London, EC1V OAT, UK

www.templarco.co.uk

Second edition

ISBN 978-1-78370-031-8

Printed and bound by Clays, St Ives plc

THE JINKS FAMILY
Me, Lucy, Mum, Dad and Stinky

For Charlie Cook, Alice Guest, Kenny Horton, Ellie Kingsbury and Kitty Smart — something to read with your dads.

CHAPTER 1

It was my hamster who woke me up, as usual. His name was Stinky and he was like a small, furry alarm clock.

I wasn't a big fan of getting up so early, but I loved Saturdays because it meant I had two whole days to spend with Stinky. Even if he was pretty grumpy sometimes.

"What do you want to do today?" I asked him, sitting up sleepily. When he didn't answer, I said, "Let's have some kind of adventure!"

He glared at me through the bars of the cage.

"An *adventure*?" he spluttered. "How exactly do you propose I have an adventure, Ben, seeing how I'm stuck in *here* all day? Oh, perhaps I could go on my wheel for a fantastic running-around-but-getting-absolutely-nowhere adventure. Or maybe I could have an incredible taking-a-nap adventure in my tiny house. Or a fun poo-counting adventure — what wonderful adventures I could have here, inside this very cage!"

He could be really sarcastic, for a hamster.

"You don't *have* to stay in there," I said. "I can get you out whenever you like."

He shuddered.

"I am most certainly *not* coming out, not when that monster might be lurking around."

The 'monster' was Delilah, my little sister Lucy's ginger kitten, and she was actually very cute. The kitten, I mean, not Lucy.

"In that book I'm reading," I said, "the kids have adventures all the time. They're called the Secret Seven — six kids and a dog who are always solving mysteries. The dog helps a lot and, unlike you, *he* can't even *talk*."

"The dog in the story," said Stinky, "is he stuck inside a cage the whole time?"

"Of course not."

"Well, then," he said. "If he were, he wouldn't be quite so helpful, would he?"

I groaned.

"Come on, Stinky. *We* could be a gang. Me and you. It would be fun. We could call ourselves the Secret Two."

"The Secret Two?" he said. "What's the big secret?"

"Well, nobody else knows that you're

4

a genius, do they? Or that you can talk. So, that's *two* secrets, straight away."

"First of all," he said, sniffily, "a gang needs more than two. Two is a *pair* or a *duo* — certainly not a gang. Secondly, the Secret Two is a rather dull name. The Secret Seven, the Famous Five — they're *good* names because the same letter starts both words. It's called 'alliteration'."

"'The Daring Duo'?" I suggested.

"Not bad," he said, "but what about 'the Tenacious Two'?"

"That depends," I said, "on what 'tenacious' means."

"It means never giving up," he said.

"In that case, I love it. *The Tenacious Two*! Now all we need is a mystery to solve."

"How about the mystery of the nine-year-old boy who didn't clean out his hamster's cage for a whole week?"

"Very funny. How about the mystery of the hamster who pooed too much and was always moaning about everything?"

Just then, though, there was a loud knock at the front door, and suddenly we didn't need to find a mystery any more.

Because a mystery came to us.

CHAPTER 2

A few seconds after the first knock came a double-knock, loud and impatient.

My dad was noisily cooking breakfast, my mum was in the shower, and my little sister was unusually quiet — not tap-dancing or singing or acting — which meant she was probably still asleep. So I bounded out of my room and answered the door.

Right away, I wished I hadn't.

Because standing there on our doorstep, for the first time ever, was Mrs Gilligan from next door, glaring down at me. I gulped.

Some of the kids on our street said that Mrs Gilligan was a witch. Her back garden was known as The Graveyard — if a ball went over her fence, it never came back.

I know that witches aren't real, of course, but she *did* look like one. She had long, grey hair, a pointy nose and was wearing a floor-length black dress. She even had an actual black cat, called Bruiser.

I held the door open, unable to speak.

"Is your mother or father in?" she

asked, impatiently.

I could only get one word out. "Dad!"

My dad came bustling out of the kitchen, with his stripy apron on and a wooden spoon in his hand. Breakfast was the

only thing he was ever allowed to cook, and even then he usually burnt something, but when he was in the kitchen he acted like he was a fancy TV chef.

"Mrs Gilligan!" he exclaimed, his eyebrows shooting up in surprise. "To what do we owe the pleasure? We're about to have scrambled eggs on toast — my own special recipe. Please join us. Come in! Come in!"

"No," she said, thin-lipped. "Have you seen my Bruiser?"

"Not recently," my dad said, still smiling. "Though he does come to our garden from time to time, hunting birds, digging up plants, burying his poos, and so on."

"I think," she said, ignoring my dad, "that he's been taken."

"Taken?"

"Stolen."

My dad had a very puzzled look on

his face.

"Why on earth would anyone want to steal Bruiser?" he said.

"What's wrong with Bruiser?" she snapped.

"Oh, nothing. Nothing at all," he said, though there was a whole lot wrong with Bruiser. "I mean, why would someone steal a *cat*?"

"I think," she said, "he's been cat-napped."

"Cat-napped?"

"Like kidnapped," she explained. "Only with a cat."

"He's probably just wandered off

somewhere," my dad said. "You know what cats are like. But if we see him, we'll let you know straight away, won't we, Ben?"

I nodded.

Mrs Gilligan scowled and marched back to her house, without saying thank you.

My dad closed the door. "Poor lady," he muttered.

"You said that she was a horrible person, before," I pointed out.

"Well, I shouldn't have said that.

She isn't always very nice, that's true. But she must be very sad and lonely. Bruiser is the only real family she's got."

Smoke and the smell of burning breakfast were wafting from the kitchen, and while my dad hurried back to it, I rushed off to my room to see Stinky.

"Bruiser next door has vanished!" I announced, breathlessly. "The Tenacious Two have got their very first mystery!"

Stinky didn't seem quite so excited, though.

"To begin with," he said, "one less cat in the neighbourhood is nothing at all to worry about. Quite the opposite, in fact. And that particular feline won't be missed by me, let me tell you." Stinky had met Bruiser once, and only just lived to tell the tale. "It is the single most unpleasant animal I've ever encountered. Who in their right mind would steal *him*? Furthermore, he is rather old, and cats often go away when they're about to die. Perhaps that's what happened. Or it's possible that he was hit by a car. Or got lost. Either way, it isn't much of a *mystery*, is it?"

But then my sister woke up, stomped

around the house for a while, and everything changed.

"Mum!" she shrieked. "Dad! It's Delilah! She's gone!"

CHAPTER 3

We all looked for the kitten — well, apart from Stinky, of course. He was having a nap.

My dad went out into the garden and searched behind the bushes on his hands and knees.

My mum went up and down the street, calling, "Delilah! Here, kitty, kitty!"

Lucy and I searched the house, from room to room

— in every cupboard, under every bed, behind every curtain. I even looked in all the kitchen drawers, in case she'd somehow got trapped there.

But there was absolutely no sign of Delilah.

My mum and dad eventually came back inside, shaking their heads.

Lucy was sobbing by now. I was used to my little sister crying, but this time it was different. I mean, she usually cried because of little things. Like, for example, if somebody had sticky-taped sponges to the bottom of her tap shoes to make them quieter (OK, that was me), or said something like, "Lucy

17

is a poo-cy" (me again). Those times, she'd burst into tears, but it was probably just an act to get me into trouble. She did a lot of acting in shows, so her performances were usually pretty convincing.

This time, though, she was properly sad. Her face was all red and actual tears were streaming down her cheeks, so I fetched her a tissue and she wiped her eyes and blew her nose. My dad beckoned me

over to him, secretively.

"Let's not mention the Mrs Gilligan thing to Lucy," he whispered.

"You mean the cat-napping?"

"Shh! That old lady's a bit crazy, and if your sister thinks that Delilah has been stolen, it will only make her more upset."

I nodded, but I doubted that Lucy could possibly get *more* upset.

Then my dad got the whole family together for a chat. We all sat around the small kitchen table, me and Dad on one side, Mum cuddling Lucy on the other.

"We're going to find Delilah," my dad announced.

"She's gone," Lucy whimpered. "Lost forever."

"Nonsense," said Dad. "She's just *misplaced*, that's all. It's like when we 'lost' the TV remote last week — remember? We finally found it in the fridge, didn't we?" (My dad himself had absent-mindedly put it in there when he got a glass of milk.)

My mum jumped up to check the fridge, just in case, but there were no cats in there, so she sat back at the table and put her arm around Lucy again.

"Delilah probably just fancied a bit of fresh air," my dad said, grinning. "That's what cats are like. She'll come back when she's hungry or thirsty. No doubt about it."

Lucy wiped her eyes and nodded. My dad was great like that — he was one of those people who always tried to stop you feeling sad. Like when I tripped over and grazed my knee, he told me a story about a man who had his *entire left leg* bitten off by a hippo. "At least you've still *got* a left knee," my dad had said to me, and it was silly, but it did make me feel a bit better.

"I once heard about a cat," my dad continued, now, "that sneaked away on a ship for a holiday, only to come back home safe and sound two weeks later." This made Lucy smile. "Or was that a dog?" my dad said, frowning. "Or it might have been a *chicken*, now I think about it."

My mum rolled her eyes at him and then looked at me.

"Ben," she said, "you and Dad go and ask all the neighbours if they've seen Delilah. Lucy and I will leave a dish of milk in the garden and wait here in case she comes back."

My dad leapt up and I followed him outside.

"If we split up," he said, "we can do this in half the time. Next-door neighbours first. Who do *you* want to ask? Mrs Gilligan or the Eggingtons?"

I didn't really want to go to either house, but I chose the Eggingtons. They were a bit less scary than Mrs Gilligan. But it was a very close thing: we had the worst next-door neighbours in the world.

While my dad walked over to Mrs Gilligan's house, I nervously edged up to the Eggingtons' front door, knocked and waited.

Edward Eggington was in my class at school and he was horrible. He was a know-it-all, a bully and a big-head, and twice he had put Stinky's life in danger. His dad was a scientist, probably an evil one, and they were always working on mysterious experiments together.

But it was *Mrs* Eggington who opened the door. She was a big woman with frizzy red hair and a frown. She said she hadn't seen Delilah, and quickly closed the door on me.

So I went up the street, knocking on doors. Everyone else was much nicer, but no one had seen a kitten.

The last house I tried was old Mr Browning's, eight doors up. He had a huge, grey moustache, was a bit deaf and was sure I was trying to sell him something.

"No, thank you," he boomed, when he opened the door. "I don't need anything."

"It's about our cat," I said.

"I *certainly* don't need a *cat,*" he said. "What would I do with a cat? No, thank you. Good day."

After Mr Browning, I'd had enough, and I hurried back home to tell Stinky what had happened.

"*Now* we've got a mystery," I said. "*Two* cats!"

"If all the cats in the world went missing," he said, "it wouldn't worry me one bit. However," he added, "it *is* a puzzle."

"It's a puzzle," I said excitedly, "for the Tenacious Two."

CHAPTER 4

The next day was Sunday and I woke up early again, still baffled by the mystery of the missing cats. Stinky was already awake, of course. He'd been thinking too, and thinking made him hungry.

"A piece of carrot would be just the thing for breakfast," he said, so I went to fetch him one.

On my way to the kitchen, I saw a white envelope lying on the carpet by the front door. I picked it up and stared at it. It was completely blank on both sides — no writing, no stamp, nothing. I hesitated, then carefully opened it and unfolded the piece of paper inside.

I´ve got your cat.
If you want to see it again
Don´t call the Police
Leave £500 in the plant pot
outside number 10

I gasped and stared at it for a few seconds longer. Number 10 was next door — Mrs Gilligan's house. Then I rushed to my mum and dad's bedroom.

"Mum! Dad!"

"What is it?" my mum asked sleepily. When she sat up in bed, I thrust the note into her hand. And when she read it, she went very pale. She nudged my dad, who was still snoring, and then shook him harder to wake him. He groaned and blinked open his eyes.

"Read this, Derek," she said, handing him the note.

When *he* had read it, he sprang up in bed like he'd been zapped.

"Blimey!" he said. "That crazy old coot was right. It *is* a cat-napper! *A cat-napper*!

Our cat's been napped!"

He leapt out of bed wearing his pyjamas, and hurriedly pulled on his dressing gown — *inside out.* Then he groped around wildly for the belt to the dressing gown and almost tripped himself up when he couldn't find it.

My mum, though, stayed calm.

"I think it's best we don't tell Lucy about this yet," she said, softly. "Derek, call the police."

"I'll just pop next door first," my dad said, clutching the note, "and see if Mrs Gilligan got one of these, too."

I followed my dad outside and then

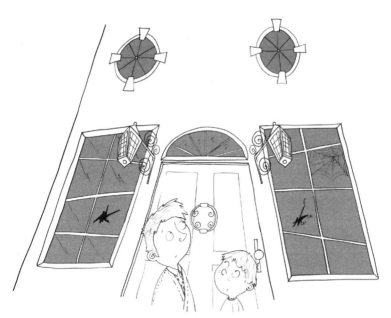

stood nervously next to him on Mrs Gilligan's doorstep, waiting. When she opened the door, I looked past her into the dark, gloomy hall. I knew she wasn't an *actual* witch or anything, but it *did* look like the kind of house where you might find a cauldron.

She didn't invite us in.

"Did you get one of these?" my dad asked, waving the note at her.

She nodded.

My dad sighed. "I'm going to call the police, Mrs Gilligan," he said. "This is a very serious business."

"Don't!" she pleaded. "The note said *not* to. If we don't do what they say, we might never get the cats back."

Her bottom lip started to wobble and it looked like she was about to cry. At that moment, I actually felt sorry for her, even though she still had two of my frisbees in her garden.

"OK," my dad said. "I won't call the police — for now."

He was a real soft touch, my dad.

CHAPTER 5

"Where's my carrot?" Stinky said, impatiently.

"Never mind the carrot," I replied, waving the ransom note at him. "I've got something that's much more interesting."

"More interesting than a carrot?" he said, frowning. "I find that very hard to believe."

I put the note down inside Stinky's cage for him to study.

"Don't poo on it,"

I said to him. "The police might need it as evidence."

He glared at me, then walked up and down on the note for a very long time, deep in thought.

The silence was driving me crazy.

"Can you believe it?" I said, excitedly. "It's an actual ransom note, like in the movies! Why *do* they cut out the letters from a newspaper, anyway? Wouldn't it be easier to just write it?"

"The police have people called handwriting analysts."

"Ana-whats?"

"Experts who can tell a lot about a

person just by looking at the handwriting."

I sighed. "Does that mean we still have no clues at all?" I asked.

"On the contrary," Stinky said. "We have a number of clues. First of all, the letters are cut from the same newspaper that your parents get — *The Chronicle.*" Stinky knew this because I used sheets of old newspaper to line his cage. (It made cleaning out his poo easier, *and* it gave him something to read.) "So," he continued, "there is a good chance that the cat-napper reads *The Chronicle,* too. When the paperboy comes, ask him who else in our street gets it."

I gasped. "You think that the cat-napper

lives on our street?"

"It's quite possible," he said. "There was no stamp on the envelope, so it must have been hand-delivered."

Stinky was like a small, furry Sherlock Holmes. *Fur-lock Holmes,* I should start calling him. Though he probably wouldn't like that so much.

"So, the cat-thieves live nearby *and* get the same newspaper?"

"Probably," he said.

"So, what do we do now?"

"We?" he said, yawning. "*I'm* going to have a little nap. But the paperboy should be here any moment. You can ask him a few questions. Why don't you go outside and wait for him?"

So I did.

The paperboy was a strange, spiky-haired, older kid called Arj, who rode a small BMX while wearing a huge newspaper bag across his shoulder.

I watched him deliver the

Eggingtons' newspaper and then ride over to our house to hand me ours. When I said, "Thanks," he just nodded. Arj wasn't much of a talker.

"Can I ask you a question?" I said.

"You just did," he replied.

"I mean, can I ask another one?"

"That *is* another one," he said.

I sighed. Being a detective wasn't going to be easy.

"Who else gets this newspaper in our street?" I asked.

"That's a very strange question," he said, but he seemed to be thinking about it. "Three houses right up there," he said, pointing to the top of the street. "Them next door," he added, pointing to the Eggingtons' house. "And her, the other next door," he said, nodding at Mrs Gilligan's house. Then he posted her newspaper through her letterbox and sped off down the street.

I ran to my room to tell Stinky what I'd discovered.

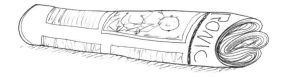

CHAPTER 6

Stinky paced up and down his cage.

"So," he said. "We have some suspects."

"Who?"

"Well, that horrible Eggington family, for a start. They live just next door, so it wouldn't be difficult for them to get the cats, would it? Perhaps Bruiser and Delilah both made the mistake of wandering into their garden. And the Eggingtons could certainly invent a cat-trap. Furthermore," he added, "they have a motive."

"A what?"

Stinky rolled his eyes.

"You call yourself a detective?" he grumbled.

"Not really," I said.

"A 'motive' is a *reason*," he explained.

"Why would *anybody* steal cats?" I asked him.

"If it *is* the Eggingtons, there are three possible reasons. Firstly, they love money, we know that. Secondly, we also know that Edward doesn't like you — and *nobody* likes Mrs Gilligan — so stealing the cats might be revenge. Finally, perhaps they stole them to perform horrible experiments on them."

My eyebrows shot up.

"Poor Delilah," I muttered. "Let's call the police."

"And tell them what, exactly?"

"That the Eggingtons stole our cat, of course."

"Hold on," Stinky said. "We don't know that it was them."

"But you said…"

"*Other* people get that newspaper, too. And the paperboy himself would have no problem getting a newspaper. You *said* he was acting strangely."

"But he *always* acts strangely."

"And he carries a big bag."

"Of course. For newspapers."

"Or cats," Stinky suggested.

Now I was *really* confused.

"Do you think that Arj the paperboy is the cat-napper?" I said.

"No," Stinky replied. "I'm just saying that it's *possible*, that's all. Detectives — *good* detectives — don't jump to conclusions. You have to consider *all* the possibilities,

44

first. However," he added, "I think we both agree that the Eggingtons are our number one suspects. But we need some evidence. You should go next door and see what you can find out."

"That will be twice in two days," I said. "They'll know that something's up."

"No one ever said that being a detective was easy," he told me.

"Hang on, Stinky. We're the Tenacious *Two*, not the Tenacious One. *You* can come with me."

He shook his head.

"If you think I am putting even one whisker into that house again, you must be absolutely crackers. The last time I was there, Mrs Eggington thought I was a rat and tried to squish me. And Edward Eggington tried to catch me and use me for a science experiment. If you remember, I was extremely lucky to escape with my life. Not to mention the talent show incident."

"But this time," I said, "you can stay in my pocket. We only need your *sniffing* ability, not your *spying* ability. You'll be able to smell any cats in the house, won't you?"

He nodded, reluctantly.

"So you'll do it?" I said.

He sighed and nodded again.

"Careful!" he snapped, as I reached into the cage. I scooped him up very gently and put him inside my coat pocket. "It's dark in here," he moaned. "And it smells of old sweets. Oh, *disgusting* — there's a crusty old tissue in here."

"Sorry," I said and took out the tissue. Then we both went next door.

CHAPTER 7

It was Edward's mum who answered the door again. She must have been cooking something, because she smelled of pepper and onions.

"You again?" she said, frowning.

"Hello, Mrs Eggington. Is Edward in?"

"He's busy with his father on a science project at the moment. But I'll call him for you. *Edward*!" she yelled. She ushered me into the house, slammed the door behind me and waddled back to the kitchen.

Stinky wriggled nervously as Edward emerged from his science lab.

"What do *you* want?" he said, not at all pleased to see me. "I'm busy."

"Busy with what?"

"Oh, I get it. You've come to steal ideas, I suppose. Well, think again. I'm working on something top secret."

I shrugged. By now, Stinky would have been able to sniff out any cats, so there was no need to stay a moment longer. I was about to turn and say goodbye when there was a noise. A *sneeze*. Coming from my coat pocket.

"What was that?" Edward said, frowning.

"What was what?"

"A sneeze. I definitely heard a sneeze."

I shook my head, and started to say, "You must have imagined it," but I only got as far as, "You—" because Stinky wriggled in my pocket and sneezed again. Louder this time.

"It's coming from your coat pocket!"

Edward Eggington said. "Something's moving in there!"

I turned to escape, but the door was closed and Edward reached out past me to make sure I couldn't open it.

"What a very odd person you are," he said, glaring at me. "Is there some kind of animal in there? Empty your pocket! Show me! Now!"

His face was turning red. I shook my head again. But now Stinky was wriggling furiously.

"It's your hamster, isn't it? Show me, or I will squash it with my hand."

He wasn't joking.

I stuck out both palms in front of me to protect Stinky, who was wriggling more and more.

Why couldn't he keep still? He was making things worse.

But then I understood what he was doing — nibbling a hole in my pocket and trying to squeeze through it, headfirst. He struggled and squirmed

and finally burst through the hole. Suddenly he was clinging onto my T-shirt, his claws poking through the material like tiny pins, jabbing into my tummy. I shut my mouth to stop a yelp escaping, and showed Edward Eggington the now-empty pocket.

He stared at it.

"The other pocket!"

I showed him that one too.

He frowned. His eyes narrowed and his mouth scrunched up in disbelief. I took advantage of his surprise to spin around, open the door and slip out.

Outside, I reached under my coat, cupped Stinky in a hand, took him back to

the safety of our room and lowered him into his cage. Both of us were shaking.

Stinky went for a run on his wheel to calm himself down. I sat on the edge of my bed and tried to slow my breathing.

"That was close," I panted, when he finally got off his wheel. "What was with all that sneezing?"

"Pepper — on Mrs Eggington."

"The big question is, did you smell any cats?"

"With all the pepper, it's hard to be sure. But I don't think so."

"What about Edward's secret science project, though?" I said. "And he *was* acting really suspiciously, don't you think?"

"That's true," Stinky said, "but I didn't smell cats, and we still have no evidence. Just the ransom note."

I scratched my head.

"I've been thinking, Stinky."

"Oh dear," he muttered.

"About the ransom note," I said. "There's something I don't understand."

"Why does that not surprise me?"

"Whoever made the ransom note," I went on, ignoring him, "they must have spent ages cutting up a newspaper so we couldn't read their handwriting, right?"

"Exactly."

"And I can understand people doing that years and years ago, before there were computers," I said. "But couldn't the person just have typed it on a computer and printed it out? You'd still never be able to work out who wrote it, and it would be much, much easier."

Stinky stared at me. For ages.

"What?" I said.

"Good grief!" he exclaimed. "You've got it! The boy has got it! My word, Ben! I think we might make a detective out of you yet!"

I looked blankly at him.

"I don't understand," I said.

He chuckled. "You might just have solved the mystery of the missing cats. Get me out of here at once!" he said, and I did. "Now, put me in your pocket again. Let's go next door."

"But we've just *been* there — and you almost got squished again."

"Not *there* — the other side. To Mrs Gilligan's house."

"Why?"

"I want to see *her* ransom note. And I need you to

ask her a few questions. Plus, this nose of mine has some serious detecting to do."

CHAPTER 8

The Tenacious Two were standing on Mrs Gilligan's doorstep. Well, *I* was standing there. I'd just knocked on the door and was waiting, extremely nervously. Stinky was twitching in my coat pocket (the one without a hole in it).

Mrs Gilligan opened the door only a tiny bit, and peered down at me through the narrow gap. "Yes?" she said, sharply. "What is it, boy?"

I took a deep breath and tried not to be scared.

"I was wondering if I could see your

ransom note, please."

"My what?"

"The note you got — from the cat-nappers."

She stared at me, her eyes narrowing.

"And why do *you* want to see it?"

"I'm — I'm investigating. I'm trying to find out who did it."

She laughed, a tiny gurgling sound.

"Investigating? You?"

I nodded.

"Have you got the ransom note?" I asked again.

She shook her head. "I threw it straight in the bin. Horrible thing. Now, shoo! I want to be alone."

Before she could close the door, though, I blurted out the second question that Stinky had wanted me to ask.

"Have you got a computer, Mrs Gilligan?"

"What?"

"A computer — have you got one?"

She squinted at me.

"Why do you ask? Are you a *burglar*, boy? Are you planning to steal things from my house? Because if I ever catch you in my house, you little wretch, I'll skin you alive!"

"No, no," I said, squirming. Stinky was wriggling furiously in my pocket, but at least he was out of sight this time, and not sneezing.

"As a matter of fact," she said, "I *don't* have a computer. Nasty, modern things. Now, instead of coming here asking stupid questions, *you* should be getting your mother and father to pay the ransom money. *Then* we can get our cats back. Now, scram!"

She slammed the door and I went back home to my room, took Stinky out of my pocket and put him onto my desk.

"What just happened?" I asked him, very confused. "Why did you want me to ask those questions?"

He beamed back at me.

"We've got it!" he said.

"Got what?"

"Our cat-napper. I know who she is!"

"She?"

"The cat-napper in question," he announced, "is none other than Mrs Gilligan herself!"

I stared at him, baffled.

"But *Bruiser* was stolen, too," I said.

"*Was* he, though?" asked Stinky. "What if he's actually in her house, right now, and she's only *pretending* he's been taken?"

"Why would she *do* that?"

"So she wouldn't be a suspect," he explained. "No one would think that *she* stole Delilah, because her *own* cat was missing."

"So *she's* the cat-napper?"

"Yes," he said. "I'm quite certain."

I shook my head. Maybe Stinky had gone crazy. Maybe *I'd* go crazy too if I was stuck in a cage all the time with only a wheel to run around on.

"Where's your evidence?" I asked him.

"Number one, there is no ransom note."

"She threw it away."

"So she says. But would she *really* throw it away? I think she never *got* one. And you were right about the ransom note, Ben. If someone had a computer, like the Eggingtons, they would have typed it up and printed it out. Only someone who *didn't* have a computer — someone like Mrs Gilligan — would need to do an old-fashioned letter using cut-up newspaper. But finally — and most importantly — when I was on her doorstep, I could smell cats."

"Of course you could," I said. "Bruiser has lived there for years and years. Of *course* the house will still smell of him."

Stinky shook his head. "I said I could smell *cats*. More than one. To hamsters, all cats have their own scent. The same goes for people. *You* smell differently from your sister, for example. In fact, while I am on the subject," he added, wrinkling up his nose, "how long has it been since you took a bath?"

"We were talking about *cats*," I said. "Not me."

"My nose tells me Delilah is in that house," he said. "She will almost certainly be shut in a room somewhere. And if your parents leave the money in Mrs Gilligan's plant pot tonight, guess what will happen?"

"She'll go out to the plant pot in the middle of the night, take the money, and let Delilah go."

"Exactly."

"So, what now?" I said. "Tell Mum and Dad, and they'll tell the police?"

He shook his head.

"They'll never believe you," he explained. "Your mum and dad, or the police, for that matter. We have no proof, yet."

"Yet?" I said suspiciously.

"Did you see her bin bag, I wonder?"

"No."

"It's on the pavement, to be collected when the binmen come tomorrow. Some detective you are," he added. "*I* was in your pocket and *I* still glimpsed it. If you look inside that bin bag, you might find an old newspaper. With some letters cut out — the letters that she used for our ransom note. *That* will be the proof we need. *Then* your parents will believe you. *Then* we'll have solved the crime."

"But if I look through her rubbish," I said, "she'll see me and stop me — and I'll be in big trouble. If there was someone small, however, who could crawl in there…"

"No, no, no, no, no," said Stinky. "No way. No chance. No."

CHAPTER 9

"It will only be two minutes, Stinky," I said. "Into the bin, get the evidence and come out."

"Why is it always *me* who gets the dangerous jobs?" he complained. "Being shot up into the sky, for example, or spying on burglars? It's your turn, this time."

"The bin bag's on the pavement right in front of her house, you said. She's always looking out of her window. She'd see me undoing the knot and rummaging through her rubbish, and then she'd go absolutely bananas. But if I walked past and dropped you on top…"

"Dropped me?!"

"I mean, very carefully *placed* you on top. Then you could nibble through the plastic and have a look inside, without her suspecting a thing. Two minutes later, I'd be back to pick you up."

"So, let me get this straight — you go for a little stroll while *I'm* wriggling about amongst putrid rubbish in the dark…?"

"You're always telling me how good your eyes are."

"Who *knows* what disgusting things might be in that bin? Rotting vegetables, sloppy old gravy, tissues with dried mucus…"

"Mucus?"

He sighed.
"The substance
that comes out of your nose," he explained,
"is called 'mucus'."

"Oh — snot?"

"Yes. Snot," he said, distastefully.

"Yuck," I said.

"And," he added with a shudder, "who knows what else might be in there?"

"In my nose?" I asked.

"In the bin!" he snapped.

"But we need the evidence. You said it yourself. We'll show it to Mum and Dad, and they'll call the police, and then we'd get Delilah back."

"Who says that I *want* Delilah back?"

It was my turn to sigh. "Remember when Lucy used to sneak in here — any time I was out — and play with you…?"

"Play with me?" he said. "Almost kill me, don't you mean? Her so-called 'cuddles' very nearly squeezed the life out of me."

"Exactly. But since she got Delilah, she hasn't bothered you at all, has she? That's why getting the kitten back will be good for you. And *that's* why you should investigate Mrs Gilligan's rubbish."

He sighed again. "OK,"

he said. "But this is the very last time I do something like this."

I wanted to hug him, but *I* might have accidentally squished him and besides, he wasn't really the hugging type. Instead, I picked him up very carefully, popped him into my pocket and we left the house straight away.

CHAPTER 10

I glanced over at Mrs Gilligan's front window as we approached the black bag of rubbish and, sure enough, she was there staring back at me.

Without breaking stride, I laid Stinky gently on top of the bin bag. It was full and didn't smell good.

He'd told me how his nose was much more sensitive than mine, but now he'd probably be wishing it wasn't.

"Good luck," I whispered, and kept walking down the street so that Mrs Gilligan would think I had somewhere to go.

After a minute or two, I turned around and walked back, really worried about Stinky. What if there was broken glass in there? Or something else sharp? He was right — he *always* did the dangerous things. Next time, it would have to be my turn.

When I walked back to the rubbish bag, I could see the tiny hole he'd nibbled through the top, but there was no other sign of Stinky. I had hoped he'd be out by now, so I could scoop him up without stopping and Mrs Gilligan wouldn't get suspicious. But instead I knelt down next to the bin bag and pretended to tie up my shoelace.

I could feel Mrs Gilligan scowling at me through the window, so I knew I didn't have long before she'd come out and shoo me away.

"Stinky!" I whispered, urgently. "Are you in there? Come out, quick!"

There was no answer. In fact, there was no noise from the bag at all.

Now I was *really* starting to panic. Maybe something had happened to him.

I'd have to tear open the bag to find him, with Mrs Gilligan watching me — and then I'd be in big, big trouble.

Just then I noticed a tiny movement inside the bag, near the bottom — the black plastic trembled, just a bit. I stared at that spot, willing it to be him. It rippled more and more. A few seconds later, a little hole appeared and Stinky burst out. My hands were shaking, but I cupped them together and held them out so he could step straight onto them. He looked awful — he was grimacing and bits of food were sticking to his fur.

As soon as he was in my hands, I

rushed him home.

"So?" I said, when I'd put him down on the desk. "What did you find?"

"A large number of things I wish I'd never discovered," he said, with a shudder. "My poor nose might never recover. Rotting bananas. Mouldy bread and rancid butter. Disgusting leftover custard."

"And?" I said, impatiently.

"And fishbones with foul-smelling pieces of fish still attached…"

"And? Any evidence?"

He nodded, and a tiny smile at last appeared on his face. "There were some pages of *The Chronicle* — all cut up."

"So, that's it!" I said, tingling with excitement. "We've solved the mystery. Mrs Gilligan *is* the cat-napper! She wrote the ransom note! You were right!"

"*We* were right."

"But wait — the evidence is still in the bin!" I said. "You didn't bring it out."

His faint smile disappeared and was replaced by a very cranky look. "Excuse me?! Did you seriously expect me to nibble my way out of the bin bag, in the dark, while holding a large piece of newspaper in my teeth?! I may be unusually clever," he spluttered, "but I am not a super-hamster. Go there and get it yourself!"

"I will," I said. "I don't care if she sees me — we *know* the evidence is there, now. I'll get it, and then everyone will believe us."

I marched out of my room and out of the house. But two paces outside our front door, I stopped suddenly. And gasped.

Mrs Gilligan's bin bag had disappeared.

CHAPTER 11

When I told Stinky the news, he groaned. "What's the plan?" I asked him.

He looked blankly back at me. "I'm trying to think, but the smell from the bin, which is currently all over my fur, is overpowering. Bring me a dish with some warm water. I urgently need a bath."

But when I came back from the kitchen with a dish full of water, he shook his head.

"Far too deep," he snapped. "I'm in need of a bath, not a *swim*!"

I went back to the kitchen and tipped some water out.

"That's better," he said, when I came back. "Hamsters are good at lots of things, but the backstroke is not one of them. Now — very carefully indeed — place me in there."

I did. He splashed around a bit to wash off the horrible smell, but he didn't look at all happy. He seemed to hate baths even more than I did.

He soon hopped out and shook himself dry, like dogs do. He was suddenly all

fluffy. It would have been funny, if things weren't so serious.

"That is the *last* time," he was mumbling. "The very last time…"

He didn't get to finish the sentence because my bedroom door creaked open, and my dad walked in.

"You gave him a *bath*?" my dad said, eyebrows raised. "Do hamsters even *like* water?"

"Not really," I said, and then I decided it was time to tell him what I knew. "I think I know who the cat-napper is, Dad."

He gave me a funny look — it was somewhere between a frown and a smile. "Who?"

"Mrs Gilligan," I said.

On crime shows on the telly, when the detective announces the name of the murderer, everyone always gasps in amazement.

My dad didn't gasp in amazement, though. He just chuckled, and ruffled my hair. "Very funny. Good one, Ben. And I suppose she stole her own cat, too, did she?"

"Well, yes, kind of."

"And do you have any proof?"

"Yes, actually. In her bin were cut-up bits of the newspaper she used for the ransom note."

My dad scratched his head. "You've been looking in her bin?"

"Yes. No. Well…"

If only I could have explained about my genius hamster, it would have been easy. But I couldn't. Stinky didn't want anyone else to know his secret — not even my mum and dad.

Dad ruffled my hair again. "*I* used to have a great imagination, son, when I was your age. And it's *great* that you're trying to find Delilah. We all are. But you can't just go around accusing old ladies — even not very nice ones — of cat theft. If you *really* want to help while Delilah's missing, you could share Stinky with your sister. You know, put the cage in her room for the night. Lucy might like that."

When my dad left the room, Stinky was furious.

"*Share* me?" he spluttered. "With your *sister*? Is he utterly *mad*? I'm not some kind of *toy*, you know. She'll dress me up in her dolls' clothes again! She'll crush the life out of me!"

"There's only one thing for it," I said. "We have to rescue Delilah!"

CHAPTER 12

Stinky went for a run on his wheel, which he often did when he was feeling stressed. When he was out of breath, he got off and paced up and down his cage, deep in thought.

Then he looked at me, and his nose twitched. Hamsters' noses twitch pretty much all the time, of course. But Stinky's nose was twitching a lot right then, and this usually meant he'd had a great idea.

"*Of course!*" he said. "Why didn't I think of it before? Lucy!"

"What about her?"

"With her help, perhaps we *can* rescue Delilah."

I stared back at him, puzzled.

"But how? Mrs Gilligan hardly ever leaves her house, and when she does, it's all locked up."

"Is it, though?" he asked, eagerly. "When she came here yesterday and you answered the door, did you notice a key in her hand?"

"No," I said. "She didn't have one."

"I thought not. And do you know what that means, detective?"

"Not really."

Stinky sighed and shook his head. "It means she didn't lock her door when she came here."

"I guess not," I said, shrugging. "We're just next door, and she was only gone a minute, so she wouldn't need to, I suppose."

"Precisely! So we have to get her to come *here* again," he explained, his eyes twinkling. "And, while she's here, *you* can go

into her house and rescue the kitten."

"Me?" I said, shaking my head. "Not likely."

"We're the Tenacious *Two*, remember?" Stinky said. "Not the Tenacious One. It seems like it's fine for the *hamster* to face danger, but when it's time for *you* to do something..."

"You heard her, Stinky. She said she'd *skin me alive* if she ever caught me in her house. And I like my skin just where it is, thank you."

"I've been *shot* into the sky in a baked bean can!" he ranted. "I've *wriggled* through bins *and* science labs and survived a night outside and…"

"OK, OK," I said. "I get your point. But how would we even get her to come here? Yesterday was the first time she's ever been to our house."

"It won't be easy," Stinky admitted. "That's why we'll need your sister to help."

"Lucy?" I shook my head again. "It's the Tenacious Two, not the Tenacious *Three*. How can she help, anyway? She's too little."

"Nonsense! I'm *very* small, and *I* help all the time. Your sister can *act*, that's why we need her. Tell her what we know about Mrs Gilligan, and about our plan to get Delilah back. She'll be shocked at first, but she'll help us. *You* need to be extremely brave, Ben. And what we need from Lucy is the performance of her life."

CHAPTER 13

Lucy was trembling as she knocked Mrs Gilligan's door. I was pretty shaky, too — peeking around the corner, out of sight. If the old lady suspected that my sister was acting, the whole plan would fall apart.

Stinky was fidgeting in my pocket. If we got inside, his sniffing ability would help me find the kitten quickly.

Mrs Gilligan opened the door and that's when Lucy's performance started. It was like she was on stage and the curtain had just gone up. She jumped up and down excitedly.

"It's Bruiser and Delilah!" she squealed.
"I think I just saw them in our garden! Come
quick! Come!"

Mrs Gilligan was frowning down at her. "Silly girl," she snapped. "Calm down. They've been *stolen*. Don't you know? They're not in your garden. You're imagining things."

"I saw them, just now!" Lucy exclaimed. "I'm sure of it! Come and look! Come quick!"

My sister was a great actor — even *I* almost believed her.

Mrs Gilligan would have known that the cats *weren't* in our garden, of course. But she must have realised how suspicious it would be if she didn't at least have a look. So, with a very impatient sigh, she followed Lucy down the passage

97

between our houses, to our back garden.

As soon as they were out of sight, I sneaked up to Mrs Gilligan's front door and pushed it. It opened.

I slipped into her house and shut the door behind me so it was exactly how Mrs Gilligan had left it — closed, but unlocked.

The hall was long and dark — the carpet and walls were a murky brown colour, with no pictures or ornaments anywhere. There were two doors on the left and two on the right, and a big, gloomy-looking room with no door at the end of the hall. I took Stinky out of my pocket so he could sniff better.

"Quick," I whispered. "There's no time

to lose. What's your nose telling us? Where's Delilah?"

"First door on the left," he said.

I twisted the doorknob and stepped into the small room.

It was a bare bathroom — with just a bath and a toilet and a sink with a dripping tap. I looked *in* the bath and *behind* it — but there was no Delilah.

I dashed back into the hall. We were already running out of time.

"Where next?" I whispered.

"She is certainly around here somewhere. My nose wouldn't let me down. Try the next door."

I flung it open and burst in. This room was much bigger. It had black wallpaper, an old wooden bed, a wardrobe and lots and lots of boxes filled with books and bottles and packages — lots of hiding places for cats. I scoured the room, jinking between boxes — looking under the bed, in the wardrobe, inside boxes, behind them. But I couldn't find Delilah.

So I stepped back into the hall, out of breath. How long would my sister be able to keep Mrs Gilligan in our garden? Not long, I was sure of that. The old lady would give up looking after a minute — after all, she knew *exactly* where the cats were.

If only *I* did.

I was standing in the middle of the hall, really starting to panic. If Mrs Gilligan came home now, she'd see me right away. And *then* what would she do? Lock me up with Delilah? Call the police? *Skin me alive*?

Stinky, on my palm, was sniffing frantically.

"Come on!" I begged him. "Quick!

Where is that kitten?"

"She's here somewhere," he said. "Right around here."

I looked around, but there was no Delilah.

"We've got to go, Stinky," I muttered.

"What was that?" he asked.

"I said, 'We've got to...'"

"No, what was that *noise*? Shh."

I spun around to face the front door, thinking that Stinky's super-sensitive ears had picked up Mrs Gilligan's footsteps. But it wasn't *that*.

It was a scratching sound, and it was coming from a little cupboard between the

two doors I'd just opened. I crouched and opened it with my free hand.

A ginger kitten — *Delilah!* — sprang out and darted through my legs. Stinky yelped in fright. I stuffed him back in my pocket, for safety, and hurried after the kitten.

"Delilah!" I said, in a loud whisper. "Here! I'm here to rescue you!"

But she just kept racing up and down the hall, no doubt relieved to be out of the cramped cupboard. I chased after her, getting dizzy myself, but I couldn't get close enough to grab her — she was probably very scared of people now. I had to keep one eye on the front door, expecting Mrs

Gilligan to come in at any moment.

Delilah dashed into the second room I'd looked in, the bedroom with all the boxes. I slipped in after her and cornered her.

"It's OK, Delilah," I whispered, kneeling in front of her. "It's me, Ben. Lucy's brother. I'm here to take you home. I won't hurt you."

I was trying to be calm but it's hard when your heart is thumping at a million miles an hour.

Delilah looked at me, and hesitated for what seemed a really long time. Then she stepped into my arms. I sighed with relief as I cradled her and turned to leave.

And that's when I heard the front door creaking open, Mrs Gilligan walking in, and locking the door behind her.

CHAPTER 14

Stinky wriggled around in my pocket. Delilah was squirming about in my arms. All I was trying to do was stay very still and very, very quiet.

Mrs Gilligan's soft footsteps were getting closer, and then suddenly they stopped. She must have noticed the open cupboard door, because she screeched:

"Drat! Where *has* that blasted cat gone?"

"Keep calm," Stinky whispered to me. "It's OK."

It was OK for *him* — *he* was hidden in

my pocket. I was in the middle of the room, with a kitten in my arms, no escape route, and a crazy old woman about to find me.

"Hide somewhere," he whispered.

I was next to the bed, so I slid under it, making sure I didn't squash Stinky or scare Delilah. I was lying on my back with the kitten on my chest, holding her with one hand so she wouldn't attack Stinky, and stroking her with my other hand to keep her quiet.

She was panting softly, but not purring. One miaow and we'd be caught.

I could hear Mrs Gilligan walking down the hall, muttering under her breath, her footsteps getting nearer. Then she came into the room we were in — the door creaked. I held my breath and turned my head so I could see her black shoes and the bottom of her long black skirt.

"Delilah!" she shrieked, and my heart pounded. "Where are you? *Bad* cat!"

Delilah was trembling. I could hardly breathe.

Mrs Gilligan walked over to the wardrobe, looked inside and then she muttered again. She looked around the room for what seemed like hours rather than a minute, and then walked out. I silently sighed with relief.

The only sounds I could hear now were Delilah's breathing and the fast beating of my heart. But Stinky had hamster-hearing, and I knew he was picking up Mrs Gilligan's faint footsteps.

"What should I do?" I whispered to Stinky. "Delilah won't stay like this much longer."

"Try to hold her until Gilligan's footsteps get further away. Then make a dash for it."

But Delilah had other ideas — she

wriggled free and shot out from under the bed.

"*Go!*" Stinky whispered. "Get her!"

I took a deep breath and slid out to where Delilah was hiding now — behind a box of bottles.

"It's OK," I whispered. "I won't hurt you."

She was still trembling but she let me pick her up.

I edged towards the bedroom door. It was open — just a bit. When I peeked out into the hall, what I saw made me jump. Mrs Gilligan was staring at me from the far end of the hall, about ten paces away, her face a horrible mixture of astonishment and fury. For a second my legs were frozen in fear. But then Delilah leapt out of my arms and sprinted down the hall to the front door and I was suddenly racing after her, with Mrs Gilligan chasing us both.

I was shaking so much I fumbled with the latch, but managed to twist it and fling the door open, burst out of the house and stumble onto the path.

Lucy came out of *our* house at the same time and gasped with delight when she saw Delilah.

Mum and Dad were behind her. My sister must have explained our plan to them as soon as Mrs Gilligan had gone back home.

My dad was completely dumbstruck. His mouth had dropped open, his eyes were wide, and he was shaking his head in disbelief.

My mum looked shocked, too, for about a second. And then she looked very, very angry. I'd seen that expression before and it usually meant big trouble for *me*.

Not this time, though.

This time it wasn't *me* she was staring at.

It was our next-door neighbour, who was standing on her own doorstep, looking very pale.

"Mrs Gilligan," my mum said, in an icy voice. "I need to talk to you. *Now.*"

Lucy came up to me, took Delilah and gave her a really, really squeezy hug.

While my mum went over to Mrs Gilligan's house to have words, my dad took me and my sister and the kitten back home.

My heart was still beating like a drum-roll.

Stinky was doing somersaults in my pocket.

CHAPTER 15

That night, I was sitting at my desk with a pen in my hand, but it was impossible to concentrate on my homework. There was too much going on in my brain, and Stinky was even more fidgety than usual.

Plus, I kept getting interrupted by my family.

My mum was first. She knocked on my door, came in and stood there, hands on hips, staring at me.

"Benjamin Joseph Jinks," she said, and I knew I was in for a telling-off — my full name only came out on special occasions.

"You did a good thing today," she continued, though I could tell from the look on her face that a 'but' was coming. "But you also did a very stupid, very dangerous thing. Imagine if you hadn't found Delilah. Mrs Gilligan would have called the police and *we'd* have been the ones in big trouble. So listen up: number one, it's definitely not OK to look through other people's rubbish."

I nodded.

"Number two, it's definitely not OK to sneak into other people's houses. All right?"

I nodded again.

"And number three, no more secrets from Mum and Dad. You got it?"

"I've got it, Mum."

"Good," she said. She frowned at me a little bit longer, and then a tiny smile broke out, just on the corners of her mouth.

"What did you talk to Mrs Gilligan about, Mum?"

"Never you mind," she said. "But you don't need to worry about her any more. Oh, and I got your frisbees back."

"Thanks Mum." I said, and she kissed me on the top of my head.

When she walked out, Stinky was staring at me through the bars of his cage.

"Not having secrets from your parents," he said, "is a very good idea in principle.

117

However, talking hamsters are a special exception, I feel."

"Don't worry, Stinky. Your secret's safe with me."

"Good," he said, "because..."

But he didn't get to finish, because my sister barged in, clutching Delilah. "Delilah wants to say thank you," Lucy said.

I looked at the kitten, but she just said, "Miaow," and didn't look especially grateful — she just looked like she wanted to wriggle free from my sister. I think she'd had enough of being manhandled for one weekend.

"I made you this," Lucy added, and handed me a thank-you card. It was brightly coloured, with a picture of me on the front and 'Ben is the Best Brother' written on it.

"Thanks," I said, and she smiled and left.

Stinky looked at the card and nodded approvingly.

"She's two years younger than you," he muttered, "and yet she's significantly better at drawing.

And her handwriting is much, much neater, too."

"Thanks," I said. "By the way..."

But this time I couldn't finish, because my dad came in.

"Are you talking to that hamster again?" he asked, grinning. "Giving him a bath, chatting to him. We should get you an *intelligent* pet — like a dog, for example. It's OK to give dogs baths, and they can understand what you're saying, some of the time. Poor old Stinky, there — his brain is no bigger than a pea, you know. And not a large pea, either."

"I don't need a dog, Dad."

"All right," he said. "Sorry I didn't believe you before, about Mrs Gilligan. I'm very proud of you, son. Maybe you'll be a famous detective when you grow up."

He ruffled my hair, walked out and closed the door behind him.

Stinky was staring at me, not looking happy. "*Dogs*?" he spluttered. "*Intelligent*? They spend most of their lives sniffing each other's bottoms, for heaven's sake! And pea-brained? That man puts the TV remote in the fridge, and he

calls *me* a pea-brain?"

I smiled.

"You solved The Mystery of the Missing Cat," I said. "Not bad for a pea-brain."

"*We* solved it," he said. "The Tenacious Two. Not bad for *two* pea-brains."

We chuckled together.

I didn't need a dog, or a cat, *or* anything else. I already had the best pet in the world.